BASEBALL BLOWUP

BY JAKE MADDOX

Text by Elliott Smith
Illustrated by Eva Morales

STONE ARCH BOOKS
a capstone imprint

Published by Stone Arch Books, an imprint of Capstone
1710 Roe Crest Drive, North Mankato, Minnesota 56003
capstonepub.com

Library of Congress Cataloging-in-Publication Data
Names: Maddox, Jake, author. | Smith, Elliott, 1976- author. | Morales,
    Eva, illustrator.
Title: Baseball blowup / Jake Maddox ; text by Elliott Smith ; illustrated by
    Eva Morales.
Description: North Mankato, Minnesota : Stone Arch Books, an imprint
    of Capstone, [2023] | Series: Jake Maddox sports stories | Audience:
    Ages 8–11. | Audience: Grades 4–6. | Summary: Malcolm loves baseball
    and science, but his teammates are not always pleased with the ideas he
    comes up with—until he uses science to come up with a winning pitch,
    the knuckleball.
Identifiers: LCCN 2022024826 (print) | LCCN 2022024827 (ebook) |
    ISBN 9781669007272 (hardcover) | ISBN 9781669007234 (paperback) |
    ISBN 9781669007241 (pdf)
Subjects: LCSH: Baseball stories. | Pitching (Baseball)—Juvenile fiction.
    | Teamwork (Sports)—Juvenile fiction. | Friendship—Juvenile fiction.
    | CYAC: Baseball—Fiction. | Pitching (Baseball)—Fiction. | Teamwork
    (Sports)—Fiction. | Friendship—Fiction. | LCGFT: Sports fiction.
Classification: LCC PZ7.M25643 Ban 2023 (print) | LCC PZ7.M25643
    (ebook) | DDC 813.6 [Fic]—dc23/eng/20220621
LC record available at https://lccn.loc.gov/2022024826
LC ebook record available at https://lccn.loc.gov/2022024827

Designer: Sarah Bennett

Printed and bound in the USA. 5195

TABLE OF CONTENTS

CHAPTER ONE

SCIENCE AT PLAY

Malcolm Morgan crouched in right field during his team's practice.

PING!

He watched as Coach Fitz hit a long drive to left field. Malcolm's teammate Walter Brill hesitated and then made his way to the ball. But the wind carried it away from him. It plopped down just inside the foul line.

"Keep your eye on the ball," Coach shouted.

Malcolm quickly tapped his smartwatch. He wore it during practice so he could monitor the weather conditions.

Sure enough, the watch said the wind was blowing at fourteen miles per hour across the field. The wind was strong enough to move any ball in the air.

Malcolm loved baseball. But he also loved science. He tried to combine the two as much as he could now that he was a Little City Lion. This wind gave him the perfect opportunity!

"Time out!" Malcolm yelled. He waved his hands to bring the outfield together.

"Guys, it's really windy out here," he said. "That's why you couldn't catch that fly ball, Walter. We should all take three steps to the right. That will put us in better positions."

"Okay, thanks!" Walter said. He trotted back to left field.

"Whatever," said Matt Staats. He was the team's best player, and he wasn't very interested in Malcolm's approach to baseball.

"But—" Malcolm began.

"You worry about yourself," Matt said, cutting him off. "I can catch any ball that comes my way."

"I'm just trying to help," Malcolm said. He shrugged as Matt stomped back to center field.

Coach Fitz cracked another fly ball, this time to center field. Matt stepped back, then forward. He sprinted to his right and . . . dove for the ball to make a spectacular catch. He threw the ball in and looked at Malcolm.

Now Coach pointed at Malcolm and hit a fly ball.

PING!

Malcolm was positioned perfectly to understand the effects of the wind. He didn't have to take a step as the ball zipped into his glove.

For the rest of practice, Malcolm was always in the right position. He didn't have any trouble, even with the trickiest fly balls.

At the end of practice, Coach Fitz called the Lions together. The whole team gathered near the pitcher's mound.

"Good work out there today," he said. "Malcolm, nice job noticing the wind conditions and adjusting. It is important to pay attention to your surroundings in a game. It could be the difference between winning and losing."

Malcolm smiled. His best friend, Sanjay Patel, walked over and clapped him on the back with his glove.

"Way to go!" Sanjay whispered as he nudged Malcolm with his elbow.

"We've got a big game coming up against the Crunch," Coach continued. "They've got some of the best hitters in the league, so I want everyone ready to play great defense."

After practice, Malcolm and Sanjay walked home together.

"I'm worried about this game," Sanjay said. "We struggled against the Crunch last time."

"I'm going to come up with something to help us beat them," Malcolm said. "Come over to my garage tomorrow and we'll work on a plan!"

CHAPTER TWO

EYES ON THE PRIZE

The next day, Malcolm opened the large overhead door to his family's garage. His parents had let him take over part of the space for a workstation. He used it to conduct his science experiments and track baseball statistics on his computer.

Malcolm was so engrossed with his latest advanced stats, he didn't notice Sanjay stroll into the garage.

"Think fast," Sanjay said as he tossed a baseball to Malcolm.

Malcolm looked up, but the light from the lamp on his garage workstation was in his eyes. He couldn't see the ball! It bonked his face and knocked off his glasses.

"Oh, man, I'm sorry," Sanjay said. "I didn't mean to do that!"

"Don't worry about it," Malcolm said, grabbing his glasses off the table. "This actually gives me an idea! We should make eye black for the game on Saturday!"

Sanjay looked confused. "What do we need eye black for? Just to look cool?"

Malcolm stood up and turned the garage light toward Sanjay. He instantly squinted.

"When you have light in your eyes, it's hard to see, right?" Malcolm said. "Well, eye black helps cut down on the glare. When you look up for a fly ball, you've got a better chance of catching it if you wear eye black under your eyes."

"Well, why don't we go downtown to Swanson's Sports?" Sanjay asked. "I'm sure we could buy some there."

"That's no fun," Malcolm said. "We can make it ourselves!"

Malcolm logged onto his computer. In seconds, he and Sanjay found instructions online for how to make do-it-yourself eye black. They just needed a cork and a lighter.

"Hang on a second," Malcolm said. "I'll be right back." Then he ran into the house to ask his dad to help.

"What are you guys up to now?" Malcolm's dad asked.

"Will you help us make homemade eye black?" Malcolm asked. Then he quickly explained what he needed.

"Okay, Malcolm," his dad replied. "Give me a sec to grab the things you need, and I'll be out to help."

When they got back to the garage, Malcolm's dad lit the bottom of the cork. After it cooled, Malcolm wiped two short, straight lines of eye black just below Sanjay's eyes. Sanjay did the same for Malcolm.

"Wow, it worked!" Sanjay shouted.

The boys ran outside to test the results. They practiced throwing the ball straight up toward the sun. The eye black made the sun seem a little less bright, and the ball seemed easier to catch.

Malcolm felt a zing of excitement. "Do you think the team will want to wear our creation?" he asked Sanjay. "It's supposed to be sunny Saturday, and there aren't many trees at the field."

"Of course!" Sanjay said. "It can only help. Plus, we'll look really cool."

The friends laughed and continued throwing the ball around.

Later that night, Malcolm added the cork to his baseball bag. His dad had said he would bring the lighter and help apply the eye black before the game.

Malcolm smiled. This was definitely his best idea yet!

CHAPTER THREE

SHINING VICTORY

Malcolm woke up Saturday and immediately opened his windows. Sunlight streamed into his room, and he pumped his fist. It was a perfect day for the eye black.

As soon as he got to the field, Malcolm found Coach Fitz, who was setting up for the game.

"Coach, I created some homemade eye black," Malcolm said. "Would it be okay if we wore some for the game today? I think it would help."

Coach Fitz looked up at the bright sun. "That's a great plan, Malcolm," he said. "We'll gather the team before we get started and see who wants some."

Malcolm ran off to find his dad.

After warm-ups, Coach Fitz addressed the Lions in the dugout.

"Listen up. Malcolm not only plays outfield and pitches for us, but he's also a bit of a scientist," he said. "He created some eye black to help with the glare today. Step right up if you want some, but don't get too carried away with it."

Nearly everyone on the team wanted to use some of Malcolm's creation. Most of the players got the standard straight line. Walter went a little crazy and made an upside down triangle shape under his eyes.

Soon, most of the team was laughing and looking up at the sun to test the results.

Malcolm looked to the end of the bench. Matt sat alone, putting on his batting gloves.

"Hey Matt, do you want to try some eye black?" Malcolm said. "I made—"

"No, I don't want to use your stupid eye black," Matt said. "I just want to play baseball without any of your gimmicks."

Malcolm stepped back. His face burned with embarrassment as Matt stormed out onto the field.

"Don't worry about him," Sanjay said. "He's just mad because he struck out twice in the last game. Everyone else is wearing it—even Coach!"

Seeing his coach wearing the eye black made Malcolm feel better. He ran to his outfield position to get ready for the game.

It turned out to be an intense matchup. The Crunch were a good team. They raced out to a 2–0 lead.

But the Lions slowly battled back. In the fourth inning, Malcolm walked and Sanjay stepped up to the plate. Leading off at first, Malcolm counted how many seconds it took the pitcher to throw the ball home.

His pitches are about two seconds slower than mine when I pitch, Malcolm thought. *Now would be a perfect time to steal a base.*

On the next pitch, Malcolm took off for second base! The catcher fired the ball to second, but the throw was high. Malcolm slid in safely. Then Sanjay followed up with a single, and Malcolm scored to make it 2–1.

In the fifth inning, with runners on second and third, Matt came through with a hard-hit double. The Lions took a 3–2 lead and held onto it until the top of the ninth.

"Great job, team," Coach Fitz said before the last inning. "We've only got three more outs to go!"

Malcolm took his spot in right field as Xavier took the mound for the Lions. The Crunch got a quick leadoff single. After a strikeout, they got another hit. There were now runners on first and second!

Then Xavier got a ground ball that could have been a double play. But the shortstop bobbled it. He threw to first for one out. Now there were runners on second and third. A base hit would give the Crunch the lead!

Xavier fired the ball in. The batter hit a high fly ball to deep center field. Matt took a step back and then put his hands out. That meant he couldn't find the ball—he had lost it in the sun!

Luckily, Malcolm had already moved toward him to back up the play. When he saw Matt panic, he ran over. The eye black helped Malcolm fight through the sun to spot the ball. He made the catch, and the Lions won the game!

The team celebrated in the dugout.

"Awesome play," Sanjay said to Malcolm.

Then Matt stomped over. "I would have caught the ball," he said. "I didn't need your help."

As Matt walked away, Malcolm and Sanjay just shook their heads.

CHAPTER FOUR

GLOVEWORK

Despite Matt's comments, Malcolm was still buzzing after he got home. The eye black had helped them win! He started thinking about an even better invention for their next game against the Dragons.

The next morning, Malcolm went to his garage and researched tips and tricks the pros used to succeed. An article about glove oil caught his attention. It said players often used oil to soften their baseball gloves. The oil helped reduce the impact of the ball and made fielding easier.

Malcolm thought that would be perfect for his next creation. He texted Sanjay to come over.

"Guess what?" Malcolm said when Sanjay arrived. "I've got another great idea to help the team win."

"Really?" Sanjay asked. "What is it?"

"Glove oil! We can put some in everyone's glove to help them field better," Malcolm said.

Sanjay hesitated a bit. "You want to make glove oil? Uh . . . I don't know if that's a great idea. Most of the team is pretty particular about their gloves."

"Yeah, I know," Malcolm said. "But this will only help! Look at this article—Devante Pierson uses oil, and he won a Gold Glove last season!"

"Well, Devante Pierson has, like, official glove oil," Sanjay countered. "Not some stuff made in a garage."

Malcolm wasn't backing down, however. "Aw, come on, Sanjay. I've got all the stuff right here. Let's give it a shot."

Malcolm held up a bottle of shaving cream and a jar of petroleum jelly. "I read that both of these can be used as glove oil," he said. "I bet combining them will make an even better glove oil!"

Sanjay scrunched his face. He still wasn't sure. "Well, I guess you were right about the eye black. Maybe we could try it."

Sanjay and Malcolm mixed the ingredients together. It made a greasy-looking oil.

"Malcolm, this doesn't look very good," Sanjay said.

But Malcolm grabbed his glove and put the mixture in the pocket of his mitt. He rubbed it in quickly.

"Let's go outside and give it a shot," he said. "I think it's going to work."

Sanjay grabbed a bat, and they went into the backyard. Sanjay hit pop-ups and grounders to Malcolm, who fielded them all. His glove didn't feel any different, but Malcolm was convinced the oil was working.

"This is great!" he said. "I'm going to bring the super-duper glove oil to the game. I can put it on everyone's gloves during warm-ups."

"No, Malcolm, you should ask first," Sanjay said. "Plus, you know Matt won't want oil in his glove. And I know I don't want any in my catcher's mitt. It's been working great for me this year."

"Okay, okay," Malcolm said. "I'll check in with everyone else first."

Malcolm knew this was what Sanjay wanted to hear, but he had made up his mind. The rest of the Lions were going to love his glove oil. He was sure of it! It would be just what the team needed to defeat the Dragons.

CHAPTER FIVE

A MAJOR ERROR

Before leaving for the game the next Saturday, Malcolm made up a fresh mix of his super-duper glove oil. He put it—and a cloth—in his baseball bag.

When he got to the field, most of the team was already warming up.

Hmmm . . . when should I try adding my oil to everyone's glove? Malcolm thought. Then he remembered the team always did a lap around the field and some jumping jacks before the game. That would be his chance!

A few minutes later, Coach Fitz gathered the team to start the run.

"I've got to fix my shoe," Malcolm said. He held up his shoe to show that the laces were all knotted together. "It'll just take a minute."

"Okay, just catch up with us," Coach said.

Malcolm quickly got to work. He applied the oil to everyone's glove except Sanjay's catcher's mitt.

When he was done, Malcolm was happy. He would tell the team about the glove oil after the game. He put his materials away and ran to catch up with the team.

The game started well. Both teams played good defense. Malcolm was excited that his glove oil was working.

But the day was hot and sunny. In the fifth inning, Malcolm looked down at his glove and noticed that it looked slick. The oil was melting!

Just then, the Dragons' hitter bounced a ball to second base. It looked like an easy play, but the ball squirted out of Jaden's glove for an error.

Malcolm's stomach started to feel queasy.

The next batter grounded to Matt, who was playing third base. As Matt threw the ball to first, it slipped out of his fingers. The ball sailed way over the first baseman's head, allowing a run to score.

When the team got back to the dugout, several players wondered what was happening.

"What's this gunk inside my glove?" Walter shouted.

"My fingers are slippery!" Anthony yelled.

Sanjay looked over at Malcolm with a surprised expression. Malcolm quickly turned his head away. He didn't want his friend to see the shame on his face.

The rest of the game was a complete disaster. The Lions' gloves caused them to make several more errors. Players began rubbing dirt in their gloves and on their hands to counteract the slickness. Malcolm could only watch in horror as they lost to the Dragons 8–3.

After the loss, the disappointed Lions gathered in the dugout. When Coach finished his words of encouragement, Malcolm raised his hand.

"Coach, I want to say something," he said quietly. "I wanted to help. So I added my homemade oil to your gloves. It was supposed to make them softer. I didn't think it would cause any problems. I'm sorry."

Everyone on the team blew up.

"WHAT!" Walter yelled.

"I can't believe you did that," Anthony shouted.

"You cost us the game with your dumb experiment!" Matt exclaimed. "And you ruined my glove!"

"Okay, everyone, calm down," Coach Fitz said. "Malcolm, what you did was wrong. Even if you were trying to help, you should have asked your teammates first. But Lions, Malcolm apologized. We all make mistakes. You can't blame our sloppy play entirely on the gloves. Let's regroup and get ready for our next game."

The team packed up their gear and left. Nobody said anything to Malcolm. He walked slowly to his parents' car for the quiet ride home.

CHAPTER SIX

BENCHED!

The Lions had a quick turnaround after the glove fiasco. They had another game the next day against the Rams. Malcolm wasn't very excited about seeing his teammates so soon. He thought they'd still be mad at him.

One of the first people he saw at the field was Sanjay.

"Hey, how's it going?" Sanjay asked as he jogged over.

"I don't know," Malcolm said. "Are you still mad at me?"

"Mad?" Sanjay said, with a puzzled look on his face. "I'm not mad. I said you shouldn't do it, but I had a feeling you would."

"What about the rest of the team?" Malcolm asked.

"You apologized, so it's all good," Sanjay replied. "I think most of the team has already let it go."

Malcolm felt relieved. At least the whole team didn't hate him. He knew Matt would still be mad, though.

As the rest of the players filtered in and sat down, Coach Fitz stood in the dugout opening. "Okay, squad, big game today," he said. "First, we need to clean up some things from yesterday's game. Malcolm, you're benched for today. I already talked with your parents about it. A team must trust each other. And even though you didn't mean any harm, going behind our backs with your glove oil was the wrong move."

Malcolm felt tears come to his eyes. He thought he might have heard Matt clap at the end of the bench, but he ignored it.

"Okay, Coach," Malcolm said, nodding his head. "I understand."

As several teammates tapped him with their gloves on their way out to the field, Malcolm decided he wasn't going to pout about the benching. He would use the opportunity to chart every pitch and play during the game. This would help him use statistics to figure out his teammates' tendencies at the plate and on the field.

As the innings rolled by, Malcolm had so much fun charting the game that he forgot he was being punished. He felt like an assistant coach. He cheered the Lions on during at bats. He talked with Sanjay about pitch selection between innings. He used his smartwatch to help Walter and Anthony be in the proper outfield positions based on the wind.

By the bottom of the ninth inning, the game was tied and the Lions had a runner on first base. As Sanjay stepped up to the plate, Malcolm had an idea!

"Coach, I think we should try doing a hit-and-run here," he said. "Sanjay has hit the ball to second base twice today. If we send the runner, that opens up a hole at second."

"Good thinking, Malcolm," Coach said with a smile. "Maybe you should take my job."

Coach gave the signal for the hit-and-run. As Walter took off for second on the steal, Sanjay ripped a line drive right where the second baseman had been standing. Then the ball scooted under the right fielder's glove. Walter came all the way home to score the winning run!

"Awesome victory, Lions!" Coach said. "And hey, let's give some credit to Malcolm. He called that hit-and-run."

The Lions all jumped around Malcolm in celebration. He felt like everyone had forgiven him. Well, almost everyone . . .

Malcolm looked around. Matt was nowhere to be seen.

CHAPTER SEVEN

CRUNCHING THE NUMBERS

After the game, Malcolm spent most of the afternoon inputting his statistics on his computer and comparing them to the rest of the season's stats. The Lions had good numbers across the board. But one stat in particular caught Malcolm's attention. He double-checked it.

Wow, Malcolm thought. *If my calculations are correct, I think I might know what to do to fix things with Matt.*

He grabbed his bike and went to correct his mistake.

Malcolm was nervous as he pulled up to Matt's house. But he needed to face his fears. He rang the doorbell. A second later, the door flew open.

"What do you want?" Matt grumbled.

"I . . . I wanted to say sorry again about the whole glove thing," Malcolm said. "I brought over some cleaner to help you fix it. I didn't make it. It's from Swanson's."

Matt relaxed a bit. "Thanks. There's still one spot I haven't been able to get clean. It's my lucky glove. I used it to make the All-Star team last year."

Malcolm and Matt sat in the front yard and cleaned up the glove. After they worked at it for a few minutes, the mitt looked as good as new.

Matt fired a ball into his glove a few times to test it. He seemed happy to have it back to normal. Malcolm breathed a sigh of relief.

"Thanks for coming over and helping me fix my glove," Matt said. "How'd you get into the science stuff, anyway? It's my worst subject in school."

"I like that science gives you a chance to explore different ways to solve a problem," Malcolm said.

Malcolm reached into his backpack and pulled out his notes.

"In fact, there's a problem I could use your help solving," he said. "I've been checking out the numbers for the team this season, and I noticed something. You've swung at the first pitch in ninety-two percent of your at bats."

"Really? How do you know that?" Matt said with a look of surprise.

"I get my dad to help me gather stats at the games, and then I put them in my computer," Malcolm said. "I think other teams have figured out your habit."

"Really?" Matt replied.

"Yep," Malcolm said. "And that's why you haven't been getting good pitches early in your at bats."

Matt thought about it. He did like to swing early. And he had been swinging at some terrible pitches recently.

"You're probably right," Matt admitted. "But I can't help it! As soon as I see the ball I want to crush it!"

"One of the things you don't want to do as a player is become predictable," Malcolm said. "You've got a pattern, and the other teams are taking advantage. But we can change that!"

Malcolm decided to find out if Matt had truly forgiven him.

"Would you like to come over and hang out with Sanjay and me after practice tomorrow?" he asked.

Matt looked at his glove. "Sure, I'll stop by. It might be fun to hang out."

As he rode home, Malcolm couldn't help smiling. He felt like maybe—just maybe—he had made a new friend.

CHAPTER EIGHT

HEAVY HITTERS

The next day, Malcolm and Sanjay walked to practice. Malcolm told him about going over to Matt's house and that Matt would be coming over to hang out after practice.

"You sure about that?" Sanjay said. "Matt's kind of intense."

"He's actually pretty nice," Malcolm said. "You'll see."

When they arrived at the ballfield, Coach Fitz looked serious. He gathered the team around him.

"Listen, we've got our biggest game of the year coming up," Coach said. "The Goliaths are in first place. They've got some of the strongest hitters in the league. They hit two home runs against the Waves last week. So, we need to play our best game of the season to win."

Practice was busy. Coach Fitz worked the team hard. They practiced several in-game scenarios. The team worked on stealing bases and hitting the cut-off man on throws in from the outfield. The stakes were high. Everyone wanted to beat the Goliaths.

At the end of practice, Coach Fitz had a few final notes for the Lions. He ended by saying, "Malcolm, it's your turn in the rotation to pitch."

Malcolm gulped. He'd have to come up with something special to beat the Goliaths. The last time he pitched against them, he gave up six runs!

"You can do it, Malcolm," Matt said. "We've got your back."

Sanjay's mouth dropped open. The rest of the team looked at each other. Did they hear that right? Matt Staats had something nice to say . . . to Malcolm?

"Thanks, Matt," Malcolm said.

After practice, Matt and Sanjay joined Malcolm in his garage. Malcolm showed Matt his statistics on the computer, and then the boys went to the backyard to play catch.

"What am I going to do to slow down the Goliaths?" Malcolm wondered aloud. "They crushed me last time."

"Yeah, it was ugly," Sanjay added. Malcolm jokingly threw his glove at his friend.

"Remember what you told me about why you like science?" Matt chimed in. "There are many ways to solve a problem in baseball too. My dad's favorite player is Jim Waveland—"

"The knuckleball pitcher?" Malcolm said. "How does that help?"

"Well, the Goliaths are expecting you to pitch the same way you did last time," Matt said. "Why not change it up and catch them off guard? Do you think you could throw a knuckleball?"

Malcolm was intrigued. He had studied how to throw a knuckleball but had never really considered using the pitch in a game. It was a pitch that went slow and fluttered unpredictably as it approached the plate. Hitters usually had a hard time trying to hit it. It was also difficult to master as a pitcher. But it would be a good way to slow down the scary Goliaths lineup.

"We're going to find out," Malcolm said. "Come over tomorrow and we'll work on it."

CHAPTER NINE

A NEW PITCH

Malcolm stayed up way too late reading, watching, and studying how to throw the knuckleball. He discovered that there were several different grips pitchers used to throw it. He also learned about the science involved in the knuckleball. The air flowing around the seams of the baseball caused it to dip or flutter as it flew toward the plate.

Malcolm spent the rest of the night holding a baseball, trying to find a comfortable grip. He watched a video of Jim Waveland teaching people how to throw the knuckler like he did.

Malcolm finally settled on a basic grip: He held the ball with his thumb tucked under the bottom of the ball and his index and middle fingers bent above the seams on the ball's backside.

Could this really work? Malcolm wondered as he drifted off to sleep, ball in hand.

* * *

The next day, Malcolm had Sanjay and Matt come over early. They took a bucket of balls to the ballfield to work on getting the knuckleball moving correctly.

Malcolm stepped onto the mound, while Sanjay got behind the plate. Matt dug into the batter's box. He was going to act as the stand-in hitter to help Malcolm see how the pitch looked to batters.

"Sanjay, this is going to be a little difficult for you to catch at first," Malcolm said. "Be ready to have the ball bounce off you."

"Okay," Sanjay said. "I also brought my brother's catcher's mitt. I read that sometimes catchers use a different glove when working with a knuckleball pitcher."

"And Matt, this is going to help you be more patient," Malcolm said. "Pretend like this is the first pitch of the at bat. Don't swing!"

Malcolm reared back and fired a fastball high and outside. Matt swung and missed.

"Hey!" Malcolm shouted. "Remember the 'be patient' plan. That was a test."

"I know, I know," Matt said. "I was just ready to hit!"

Now Malcolm was going to try the knuckleball. He got the grip right and flicked the ball toward the plate. But nothing happened. It was a straight, slow pitch right into Sanjay's glove. Malcolm threw a few more. The knuckler wasn't dipping.

On pitch seven, Malcolm adjusted his fingers a little bit and let it fly. Matt took a big swing and missed.

"Whoa!" Matt shouted as his knees buckled. "That was amazing! The ball moved all over the place. I didn't know where it was going!"

Malcolm kept throwing the knuckleball. Some of them danced in the air and dropped to the ground as Sanjay tried his best to catch them. Some of Malcolm's pitches came out flat, and Matt hit those ones hard.

When the bucket was finished, Malcolm guessed that about half his knuckleballs worked the way he wanted.

"What did you guys think?" Malcolm wondered as they collected the balls.

"I thought it was great," Matt said. "As a hitter, I couldn't track where the ball was going. It was hard to time it up."

"I think if we mix these in with your regular pitches, we can keep the Goliaths guessing," Sanjay added.

Malcolm wasn't so sure. It was a big deal to try a new pitch, especially in such a huge game. What if this experiment failed?

CHAPTER TEN

KNUCKLE DOWN

Malcolm woke up early the day of the game. He kept testing his grip and throwing practice pitches into a net in the yard. By the time he got to the ballfield, he thought he was ready to unleash his knuckleball on the Goliaths.

But then he got a look at the crowd. It was packed! The Goliaths' side of the field was filled with fans. Even the Lions' side was crowded. Malcolm saw several friends from school in the crowd, and a lot of them didn't even like baseball. He was going to be front and center.

"Are you ready to give them the ol' knuckler?" Sanjay said.

"I guess so," Malcolm said shakily.

The Lions were at bat first. Xavier led off the game with a hit, and then Walter struck out. With Matt batting next, Malcolm gave him one final piece of advice.

"Be patient," he said. "Don't swing at the first pitch."

Matt strolled into the batter's box. The Goliaths' pitcher wound up and fired the ball. Matt flinched like he was going to swing, but he held back as the ball went low and outside. He turned to Malcolm, who gave him a thumbs-up.

Matt settled back into the batter's box. The Goliaths' pitcher looked in for the signal. He wound up and fired a fastball right down the middle. *CRACK!* Matt blasted it to left field for a run-scoring single.

By the bottom of the first inning, Malcolm took the mound with a 1–0 lead. Suddenly, he wasn't so sure about throwing the knuckleball.

Maybe I'll start with a fastball, he thought. He looked for Sanjay's signs. His friend called for a knuckleball. Malcolm shook his head. Sanjay then put down the sign for a fastball. Malcolm nodded. He wound up and fired . . .

CRUNCH! The Goliaths' leadoff hitter smacked it up the middle for a single.

Okay, they just got a little lucky, Malcolm thought.

Sanjay called for another knuckleball. Malcolm nodded away the sign again. He wanted to try another fastball. He wound up and fired.

CRACK! The next hitter crushed the ball to deep left field for a double, and the score was tied 1–1.

"Time!" Malcolm heard from behind him. Matt jogged over. "I thought you were going to throw the knuckleball?"

"I don't know, Matt," Malcolm said, rubbing the sweat off his brow. "What if it doesn't work?"

"Trust the science, Malcolm," Matt said. "That's your thing, remember? I know you can do it."

Malcolm gathered himself. He looked at Sanjay and nodded. He gripped the ball and threw the knuckler. It drifted and hit the batter! Now there were two runners on base and no outs.

Malcolm felt bad, but the ball had moved a bit. He decided to throw another knuckleball. This one danced and fluttered to the plate.

WHIFF! The Goliaths' hitter took a huge swing and missed.

Malcolm continued to mix his fastball and his knuckleball. To his relief, he managed to get out of the inning without allowing any more runs.

"What are you throwing out there?" Coach Fitz asked when Malcolm ran to the dugout.

"My super-duper knuckleball," Malcolm said. "Do you like it?"

Coach chuckled. "Whatever works."

For the next few innings, Malcolm kept the Goliaths off-balance with his mix of knuckleballs and fastballs. They swung way too early on the knucklers and way too late when Malcolm sped up the pitches.

By the bottom of the ninth, the Lions were clinging to a 2–1 lead. Sanjay had driven in the go-ahead run with a sacrifice fly in the seventh inning. As Malcolm walked out to the mound, he could feel the pressure to pick up the victory.

The last half of the inning started out well. Malcolm struck out the leadoff hitter. But then the next Goliaths batter hit a hard double.

Malcolm felt a little anxious. As the crowd went wild, he wound up and threw a fastball. *PING!* The Goliaths hitter drove the ball foul down the third baseline.

Malcolm's next knuckler bounced off the plate and away from Sanjay. The runner moved over to third.

Malcolm was worried about throwing the knuckleball. He was happy when Sanjay signaled for a fastball. He threw one right to the outside corner.

"STRIKE!" the umpire bellowed.

The count was one ball and two strikes. Malcolm leaned in, and Sanjay called for the knuckleball.

Malcolm let it fly. It was perfect—the best knuckler he'd thrown all day.

WHIFF! The batter swung and missed for the second out. But the ball ticked off the top of Sanjay's glove and rolled away.

Seeing a chance to score the tying run, the runner at third took off down the line. As Malcolm sprinted to cover home plate, Sanjay recovered the ball. Then he flipped it to Malcolm, who slapped his glove down to tag the runner.

"OUT!!" yelled the umpire.

Just like that, the Lions won the game!

"Way to go!" Matt shouted as he ran in from third base. "The knuckleball worked!"

Malcolm beamed as Matt, Sanjay, and the rest of the team carried him off the field. Science, statistics, and a whole lot of teamwork had saved the day!

AUTHOR BIO

photo by Elliott Smith

Elliott Smith has written more than 40 chapter books for young readers in a variety of topics. He previously worked as a sports reporter for newspapers. He lives in Falls Church, Virginia, with his wife and two children. He loves reading, watching sports, going to concerts, and adding to his collection of Pittsburgh Steelers memorabilia.

ILLUSTRATOR BIO

photo by Eva Morales

Eva Morales is a professional 2D illustrator and artist living in Spain near the Mediterranean Sea. She worked in children's publishing, TV, film production, and advertising for about fourteen years. Now she works as a full-time freelance illustrator, using a combination of digital and traditional techniques. Eva loves to walk on the beach and read books in her spare time.

GLOSSARY

anxious (ANGK-shuhss)—afraid or nervous about what might happen

fiasco (fee-ASK-oh)—a complete failure

gimmick (GIM-ik)—a clever trick or idea used to get people's attention

glare (GLAIR)—very bright light

lineup (LINE-uhp)—a list of players taking part in a game

patient (PAY-shunt)—calm during frustrating, difficult, or exciting times

position (puh-ZISH-uhn)—a player's role or place on a field of play

pressure (PRESH-er)—a burden or strain

queasy (KWEE-zee)—an uneasy or troubled feeling

scenario (suh-NAH-ree-oh)—an outline of a series of events that might happen in a particular situation

statistics (stuh-TISS-tiks)—the science of collecting numerical facts, such as a baseball player's achievements on the field

technique (tek-NEEK)—a method or a way of doing something that requires skill

DISCUSSION QUESTIONS

1. Why do you think Coach Fitz let Malcolm try some of his unique strategies during practice and games?

2. Why was Matt so upset about Malcolm's experiments and inventions?

3. Do you think Sanjay was nervous about having to catch a new pitch in the big game?

WRITING PROMPTS

1. Malcolm combined his love of science and baseball to have fun. Write about a time you combined two of your passions. Describe what you did and how it worked out.

2. How would you feel if you altered your teammates' equipment and it cost you a game? Pretend you're Malcolm and write an apology letter to the team.

3. Have you ever been too scared to try something difficult? Write about a time you overcame your fears and did something that was uncomfortable.

SCIENCE AND MATH IN BASEBALL

Baseball is definitely a fun game to play with your friends. But you can also use science and math to create a deeper understanding of how the game is played. You may not realize it, but every time you play catch, several principles of science are on display!

Newton's First Law of Physics says an object at rest won't move without an outside force. When you pick up a baseball and throw it, the force of your arm gives the ball momentum. And then the energy of that momentum is transferred to the glove that catches it.

Statistics are a critical element of baseball study. Some stats, like batting averages, can be computed using simple math (number of at bats divided by hits), while others are calculated by complex computer programs.

In Major League Baseball, the pitcher's mound is 60 feet, 6 inches from home plate. According to scientific study, the batter has about 0.09 seconds after the ball leaves the pitcher's hand to determine whether to swing or not.

Players now use infrared cameras, motion technology, weighted baseballs, and other high-tech tools to acquire valuable data that can help them gain an advantage on the field. Science is now as big a part of baseball as bubble gum!